TERRAFORMA

CONNOR WHITELEY

No part of this book may be reproduced in any form or by any electronic or mechanical means. Including information storage, and retrieval systems, without written permission from the author except for the use of brief quotations in a book review.

This book is NOT legal, professional, medical, financial or any type of official advice.

Any questions about the book, rights licensing, or to contact the author, please email connorwhiteley@connorwhiteley.net

Copyright © 2024 CONNOR WHITELEY

All rights reserved.

DEDICATION

Thank you to all my readers without you I couldn't do what I love.

CHAPTER 1

"Why doesn't the Empire terraform planets?"

Dr Aaron Lawrence had always been fascinated by that simple question ever since he started studying plant biology over forty years ago, and it turned out absolutely nobody knew why. Not his professors, not Aaron's best friends or bosses in the Plant Biology Centres that seemed to both be everywhere and nowhere in the Empire, and not even the researchers at the Emperor's own research labs seemed to know.

Aaron flat out couldn't understand why such an advance civilisation like The Great Human Empire that definitely had the technology to terraform entire worlds, sectors and the whole galaxy, they simply didn't use it.

As Aaron sat on the perfectly warm metal seat with blue fabric lining its soft cushions of the private blade-like shuttle as it descended out of orbit of the planet Terraforma, Aaron was getting more excited about this brand-new research trip that he had been especially requested for.

Aaron had never travelled by private shuttle before and it was amazing. Normally he was stuffed into the long metal tube of a shuttle shoulder-to-shoulder with dirty poor plebs of the Empire that were more focused on finding their next meal than learning about the mysteries and secrets of the universe.

Of course Aaron helped them whenever he could and Aaron was always a thousand credits poorer by the time he left the shuttle just so he could help those poor people, but this private shuttle was simply wonderful.

The air was so much better with its hints of mint, pine and moisture that most shuttles in the Empire simply pretended wasn't there. Normally all Aaron could smell was sweat, urine and even poo from the other poor people but thankfully private shuttles didn't have that problem whatsoever.

Even the long metal tube with its bright and shiny silver walls were amazing compared to the normal ones on normal shuttles. It wasn't dirty, covered in dust or anything. And it was so much quieter because on normal shuttles Aaron guessed that the enviro-systems needed to work overtime to make sure the dust and dirt didn't get into the cockpit where the high-tech instruments were.

The almost silence of the shuttle was a little strange and Aaron had hated it for ages so he had hummed a few tunes to himself and murdered a good few popular songs.

Aaron always loved going out to clubs, bathhouses to see what hot men were about and socialising with his friends. It was his friends that were the highlight of his life and as much as he loved his work and was dedicated to it, he really did love his friends. It was just a shame that they were on the other side of the Empire living their own lives, with their own families and Aaron was almost alone in the fact that he was still single.

Thankfully because Aaron was very rich because of his academic books, papers and lecturing he could easily afford high-quality rejuvenation treatments so he didn't look a day over thirty, like so many people in the Empire.

Yet it still would have been nice to have a man in his life.

"We'll be docking in twenty minutes Doctor," a woman said over the ship's intercom system, "and very nice singing,"

Aaron just grinned. It had forgotten that shuttles had hidden cameras to monitor the cargo. Aaron really wanted the ground to swallow him up he wasn't a good singer and he knew it.

Well, at least it wasn't like he was going to ever see that woman again so he hopefully didn't need to be embarrassed too much longer.

Aaron really hoped that the female pilot would put down his bad singing to his "academic casual" look of black jeans, a white shirt and hiking boots. It made him all just enough like an academic for people to take him seriously but not so much that people wanted to run away from him at first-sight.

And in Aaron's experience academics simply couldn't sing, dance or drink very well.

Aaron felt his stomach get more and more excited at the idea of docking in only twenty minutes time because he would finally discover who he had summoned him exactly and most important why had they.

All Aaron knew about the people requesting his present was that his boss seemed to love them because he was more than happy for Aaron to go and help them. These people were clearly rich-rich because they had said they would pay for every single little expense of the trip, even if Aaron wanted to stock up on sweets before he came here.

Of course Aaron didn't but it was still a nice gesture.

And Aaron knew that they had head-hunted him because his research focused on the Empire's terraforming efforts. He had barely made any progress since his doctoral thesis which was why he mainly focused on studying alien plants and crops these days, but now that he had actually been given access to the world of Terraforma Aaron also knew that these people had to be very influential on Earth.

Aaron had tried to get access each week to Terraforma because it was the only world that was known for the Empire trying to Terraform it. Having access to the world would have helped his doctoral thesis massively but each week Earth sent him a personal rejection that after a month turned into a form rejection.

There was no way in hell that Aaron was getting access to Terraforma but now Aaron couldn't understand what had changed and why someone wanted him to research it.

As Aaron felt the shuttle start to dip and descend faster towards the docking bay, Aaron felt more and more excited. He just knew that this was going to be the start of an amazing adventure that would be filled with mystery, excitement and plenty of secrets.

CHAPTER 2

Doctor Callum Buck sat on a large grey metal platform with plenty of little metal hovering tables, chairs and people organised in neat little rows overlooking an absolutely stunning mountain range. The people sitting at the little tables were mainly all posh snobs of the science, political and military worlds that saw Terraforma as their holiday home.

Callum had never been keen on coming to Terraforma before because he was a geologist by trade and loved focusing on the geographical forces that played, shaped and manipulated a planet's surface to create the structures and formations that everyone saw today.

Callum watched the other people at the table closest to him, they were a wonderful young couple who looked like they had just made professor at their university judging by the happiness, youthfulness and sheer ignorance on their faces. They were wearing a wonderful black dress for the lady and a freshly pressed blue suit for the man.

The man looked really hot and Callum had to force himself not to keep staring because the man was just sheer perfection. But he also forced himself not to go over to the table and give the two new professors some tips about how to survive university politics, departmental wars and all the hidden things that happened behind closed years.

It was a sheer nightmare and Callum was so glad that he had given up university lecturing a few decades ago. And now he researched his own academic textbooks, wrote them up and occasionally consulted for the Martian Government about how the geography of a planet would impact their Forge World operations.

Callum wasn't exactly sure if he enjoyed consulting for Mars very much because the Martians were just weird, cold and not human at all. But they were part of the Empire and that was good enough for him at times.

Callum forced his attention away from the cute man and his girlfriend and wrapped his hands around his own large piping hot mug of spiced coffee. Callum loved the sweet hints of vanilla, Cocait (a local form of the coca bean that was only found on Terraforma) and the rich spiced flavour of the cinnamon.

It was amazing how the ingredients on the world seemed to be richer, thicker and have a more intense flavour than those on other worlds. Of course there were numbers of geographical factors that could impact the flavour and Callum was really excited about finding out and researching them all.

"Our guest should be joining us shortly," a woman said.

Callum smiled at his best friend and old professor Doctor Luna Goodman, who was wearing a thin black jumper, some hiking boots and black trousers. Callum had known her for so long that it was brilliant to see her again and it was really kind of her to invite him on this trip of hers.

"They ran out of coffee pods dear," a man said, "but the hotel receptionist will make a note of it and get the food synthesisers updated in the room,"

Callum smiled and his mouth dropped when he saw that Professor Eli Newport was joining them for this meeting, he might have been married to Luna but he was a legend in the biology community and he had a very good foothold in the history community as well.

Both of their work was revolutionary in more ways than one and Callum felt so privileged to be able to see them both, talk with them and actually have breakfast with them. Callum had to admit that he sort of felt like a dumb child compared to these divine researchers.

In an effort to make his brain return to working normally in the presence of these amazing people, Callum looked out over the stunning mountain range. The hotel and resort they were staying at was on the highest peak on the entire planet and there was a large oxygen shield around the resort to make sure they didn't suffocate up here.

Callum could see hundreds of miles all around and it was stunning to see all the fold mountains rising up from the ground like daggers and scratches that had shaped the land over thousands of years.

But if the legends were believed then normally whilst fold mountains took thousands of years to become mountains, these mountains had only taken a day because of the Empire's terraforming efforts.

Something they never repeated again and that was just fascinating to Callum.

"Menus," Luna said and moments later four holographic menus appeared in their hands and Callum really loved this expensive resort.

Callum already knew exactly what he was going to have for breakfast because he was at such an exclusive mountain resort, he was going to have what everyone in the Empire would have if they came here. He was going to have the Emperor's Breakfast, an immense plate of all the richest, creamiest and most indulge food that had been sourced across the rest of the Empire.

He had no idea if this was what the Emperor actually had for breakfast each morning, he probably didn't, but it was great marketing.

"Wow," Eli said. "Our guest is here early,"

Callum watched as Eli got up and went over to greet the guest and Callum was taken away slightly. This man was... breathtaking.

Callum felt so underdressed in his white t-shirt, black jeans and black trainers. He was having breakfast, not going to a banquet at a university but this man was so hot and sexy and wow, Callum was really struggling to keep his body in check because the man was so divine looking.

Callum's wayward parts flared to life instantly and he could feel his brain melt inside him. He really loved the man's pointy handsome face that showed a wonderfully strong jawline, deep orange eyes that looked radiant in the sun and the man just looked like he had fallen from heaven as the Old Earth legends used to say.

The man was so perfect that Callum knew that he was going to enjoy this project a lot, lot more than he felt like he had the right to.

CHAPTER 3

Aaron was completely amazed that he had somehow managed to make his way over to the small hovering table, and he was more than glad he was actually sitting down now because his legs had turned to jelly, his brain was mush and his mouth was sucking all the energy from his body because he didn't dare allow his mouth to drop.

Aaron had seen a lot of hot men in his life but none were as beautifully perfect as Doctor Callum Buck. Especially as he sat there so confidently, sexy and just like he owned the entire immense metal platform they were sitting on.

There was just something about Callum's longish brown hair that was styled over itself and parted to the right, his smooth handsome body and amazingly fit body that told him that Callum worked out like him. He probably lifted some weights, ran a lot and Aaron just smiled more and more thinking about it.

Callum just had to be the most amazing and

stunning man he had ever met.

Aaron forced himself to look away from the perfectly wonderful man sitting next to him and he looked at the not-quite-so-stunning mountain range. It was immense and extremely impressive how the geographical forces of Terraforma could have caused this to happen.

Aaron knew a little about geography and earth sciences but the mountains just weren't that interesting for him because they was plenty of snow that blanketed the mountains, but he highly doubted there were any plants underneath it.

He didn't know why he was here at all.

The sound of other people talking and saying how great their food was and wonderful to hear was strange after the eerie silence of the shuttle, and Aaron was so looking forward to exploring the project or whatever they were here for with perfectly stunning Callum.

"Now that both of you are here," Luna said, and Aaron felt his brain start to turn again in front of these amazing professors, "we want to offer you both a job,"

Aaron nodded because at least that now explained the very standard and to be honest rather low-risk non-disclosure agreements they had to sign before they boarded the shuttle. Well at least Aaron had to do that.

"And just a reminder that whatever we discuss from this point forward cannot be discussed with anyone else," Eli said.

Aaron nodded and it sounded completely okay and very standard for science work, but it wasn't standard when Eli took out a very little black sphere, tapped it on the table and silence filled the air as the device created a sound shield around them.

Aaron was glad to see that Callum also looked unsure. "This is getting a little weird,"

Both Luna and Eli laughed. "Yeah. Tell me about it and it's only going to get weirder, because do you two know why no one is allowed to leave the hotel complex and go further north on Terraforma?"

Aaron shook his head and he really wanted to say something intelligent but he couldn't. His brain wasn't functioning because he had heard about that black sphere device and its use was extremely rare and he had no idea how two amazing professors had gotten it.

"Because the entire planet is under Empire Restrictions," Callum said. Aaron really loved the sound of his manly voice.

"Yes," Luna said, "and we have been authorised by the Inquisition to research why Empire Terraforming efforts didn't go beyond this planet,"

Aaron's eyes widened and Callum gasped. It was incredible to imagine that the top-secret organisation known as the Inquisition, the organisation that answered only to the Emperor and had the power to erase people from history, burn entire worlds and be a law onto themselves was asking them to do this.

Eli smiled. "Yes, it was a rather big shock to us too but if you want to join us then the research permits and certificates will be sent to your personal dataslates as proof, and the Inquisition has even allowed us to publish our research in whatever journals we want,"

Aaron just looked at the extremely hot man sitting next to him. He had never ever heard of such a sweet deal in all his life, and he had never heard of the Inquisition being so desperate for information that they would allow it to be shared.

"You don't have to answer us right now but I would like an answer before lunch please just so we can start planning the trip because we both would like to start tomorrow morning," Luna said.

"Also it is perfectly okay for you to deny and turn us down. In return we simply ask you to stand by the non-disclosure agreements," Eli asked.

As much as Aaron wanted to bait them a little and pretend that he wasn't interested. This was a stunningly good opportunity and it would make them the only four researchers in all of human history to research Terraforming in practice, something that had never been done before.

Of course some researchers had tried to do it but their articles were dismissed as being unempirical, crazy and a failure and they were always right. Aaron had a chance to take it and truth be told he really wanted a few more days, weeks or months to get to know this stunningly hot man next to him.

Aaron just wanted him to be into men and as Luna and Eli went off to have their breakfast inside as they apparently had some paperwork to do, Aaron's stomach churned, flipped and filled with excitement at the very idea of spending alone time with this hottie.

This trip was going to be amazing.

CHAPTER 4

Callum seriously couldn't believe how sensational the breakfast was and it was funny how all four of them had ordered the Emperor's Breakfast, which made him feel a lot better about ordering it because of how expensive it was. Just one breakfast was the same as most Empire workers earned in a month.

Thankfully Luna and Eli had left him and sexy Aaron alone, and even now Callum was fighting the urge to ask him out or something because of how great the morning had been so far.

The wonderful flavours of freshly roasted pork, crispy salty bacon and the most sensationally juicy sausages left the most incredible taste in Callum's mouth, and this breakfast was certainly worth the money. It was amazing.

The morning had also been great because it had given him and sexy Aaron the perfect chance to talk, get to know each other and think about the project. They hadn't spoken much at all about the project because Callum had been fascinated with how Aaron had gotten into plant biology and it was so refreshing to hear someone as passionate about their subject as he was.

It was actually why his relationships tended to fail one by one because it seemed that no man could put up with his intense focus and weird little ways, like getting lost in thoughts whenever he was focusing so much on a problem.

Callum loved talking to Aaron because he really was so intelligent, kind and he made Callum feel a lot more normal when he mentioned that he also donated millions each month to charities because they both didn't need their millions all the time.

It was impossible for Callum to believe that there was or would be anything that he wouldn't like about Aaron because he really was perfect, and it was clear as day how into Callum Aaron was and Callum didn't have a problem at all with that.

And even now as Aaron sat there finishing his breakfast, drinking his coffee and smiling like he was a teenage boy on a first date (Callum suspected he looked the exact same way), Callum had to admit that Aaron looked so divine in his white shirt and black jeans.

"What do you think about the project?" Callum asked as he took a large delightful mouthful of his richly spiced hot chocolate.

"To be honest, if I can keep having breakfasts like this one, spend more time with you and work with Luna and Eli. Then I would do anything,"

Callum laughed because he felt exactly the same. Their two heroes of their science community were giving them the chance of a lifetime and this was definitely going to define their careers.

That had some positives and negatives because if they succeeded then they would go down in history as some of the most famous scientists in all of human history, but if they failed then there was a good chance that their reputation would certainly take a hit.

And even the little fact that they had been given this opportunity in the first place, that would definitely impact their popularity and would make them enemies. Then those enemies would probably go out of their way to make sure Callum and beautiful Aaron didn't get access to grants, job promotions and journal publications.

This job had massive risks but Callum didn't care. He was rich and he was never going to pass up the opportunity to work with Luna and Eli and spend more time with such a hot man.

"What do you know about Terraform?" Aaron asked, finishing up a sausage.

Callum couldn't help but grin because his mind was going to dirty places. "Not much. Most records about Terraforma are off-limits to everyone in the science community so whatever happened here had to be big,"

"Especially if the Inquisition don't have access to it," Aaron said. "We know they have access to everything in the Empire so why not these records?"

"They were probably destroyed," Callum said and he really didn't like to admit it. It was such a horrible crime to him that someone would actually destroy historical records that could be so critical to the future of humankind.

"The Empire only destroys records if something went very, very dangerously wrong. You still want to do this?"

Callum loved how Aaron was smiling and they both laughed because that was a stupid question. The danger only made them want to do this even more.

"Now before we go and tell Luna and Eli about our decision," Callum said leaning forward. "Please tell me more about your bathhouse experiences, the worlds I visited as a young man didn't have that?"

Aaron gave Callum a devilish smile and ordered them two more mugs of hot chocolate from the food synthesisers and Callum was really, really looking forward to spending more time with this hunk of a man.

CHAPTER 5

As Aaron, with Callum very close behind him, went into a large private room in the resort with large windows that were waist height, giving him plenty of great views of the stunning mountain ranges and the thick blanket of snow veiling the land, Aaron couldn't believe how excited he was that Callum was into him and gay.

Aaron had absolutely loved their breakfast with their intelligent refreshing conversation that he never could have had with his past boyfriends. Callum was just perfect, caring and seemed to love science just as much as him.

And their more sexual conversations had been even better, filled with laughter, stories and Aaron just felt like he really, really knew what Callum was like behind his white t-shirt, jeans and trainers, and Aaron seriously liked what he knew.

Aaron liked that Callum was staring out the large

windows and he would have loved to know what he was seeing. Callum was probably seeing thousands of years worth of geographical processes just like how he saw millions of biological processes whenever he saw a plant.

He forced himself to stop staring at the hot sexy man he was falling for and he pulled out a black metal chair that sat around a grey metal conference table that sat in the centre of the room.

The ceiling was covered with the sensors of holograms, security cameras and food synthesisers so at least if they were going to be in here all afternoon then they were going to have plenty of food and drink available to them. Aaron was more than glad about that. He had been in too many academic seminars over the decades without food and drink and they never ended well.

A few moments later Luna and Eli grinned as they walked in wearing blue business suits that really flattened their bodies, and Luna clapped her hands and a large blue hologram of Terraform appeared as if viewed from orbit.

Aaron was amazed at how great it looked with the snowy, mountainous region they were in at the very bottom of the planet, and then dry deserts, rainforests and other biomes littered the rest of the planet.

He might have been a plant biologist by trade but Aaron loved studying how the geography of a place caused only certain plants to grow and develop adaptations so they could thrive in the environment.

"You two should see your faces," Luna said grinning.

Aaron smiled at them all and then they all sat very close to each other and the cold metal chairs.

"I take it you're going to accept the job offer?" Eli asked.

"Of course," Callum said and Aaron nodded.

"Brilliant, and you doubted them Luna," Eli said, and Luna playfully hit him. "So now we want to explain what our plan is and we want your honest feedback. If there's a problem or an area for improvement, tell us because it's why you're here,"

Aaron nodded but he seriously couldn't imagine what he could see that the two greatest minds of the Empire couldn't.

"As you know we're currently in the south of Terraforma and our estimates and preliminary research shows that the geographical formations here are newer than the ones further north," Luna said.

"So you believe the terraforming started further north for example," Aaron said, amazed his brain managed to work.

"Yes," Eli said. "Now our early research shows that the rainforests in the northeast regions of the planet are the oldest formations on the planet. Followed by the Temperate deciduous forest, you know how legend describes living in Europe and North America from Old Earth, and then the desert were created,"

Aaron was really impressed with the research so far but he understood why these two great people had called him and Callum in, because they had spent ages calculating this data and this was as far as they had gotten.

"And you didn't see any dangers or reasons-" Aaron was about to ask.

"Well, that's the problem," Eli said. "We calculated all this data with probes and we have never left this resort. All our data is correct regardless of scientific calculations used but we haven't been outside yet,"

"Oh," Aaron said and flinched as he realised that he had just insulted the two best minds of the Empire but they nodded. At least he wasn't in trouble this early on in the trip.

But this was a massive problem and Aaron was surprised that these two hadn't got outside. Then again they probably weren't allowed to but they were going to go out now into the wilds of Terraforma without knowing what creatures or flora they might face.

There was a reason why the Empire destroyed the records and that reason couldn't be safe.

"We want to travel to the rainforests first of all and start our studies there because that seems to be the starting point of the terraforming efforts, and that should start us off on the right track," Eli said.

Aaron agreed with the idea but something felt off about it. Given how the aim of terraforming was to make a planet like Earth and make human habitation easier for people, it made no sense to start off with the rainforests. As the people of Europe and something called *North America* had discovered on Old Earth, forests were the easiest to live in.

Why not start there?

"What are we looking for exactly?" Callum asked and Aaron nodded to second the question.

"We, we don't know," Luna said. "This is why we wanted a plant biologist with us and a geographer by trade. We needed two intelligent people to help us understand this mystery because this planet is why the Empire doesn't Terraform planets and we want to know why,"

Aaron could only nod in agreement. This planet was probably one of the most important planets in the history of the Empire from a science viewpoint and the very idea that they were going to explore the unknown really excited him.

And really terrified him at the exact same time.

CHAPTER 6

After a wonderful afternoon of talking shop, discussing how the terraforming technology would interact and reshape the natural geographical processes of the planet and enjoying even more time with sexy Aaron, Callum had to admit that he was in absolute heaven. And as much as he had wanted to take Aaron straight into his bedroom last night, he had forced himself not to.

Yesterday had been the best day of his life and as Callum stepped out onto the soft wet ground of the rainforest he was really looking forward to the rest of the trip. Luna and Eli had hired a private shuttle to fly them the four-hour journey from the resort to the very centre of the rainforest and that had given them all four hours to check their equipment, make sure it all worked and that they were all ready.

Callum had always loved rainforests since he was a teenager who first visited one as part of a school trip, and this rainforest seemed to be even more perfect.

The immense ancient trees rose up into the sky like people reaching out of the ground hoping to grab a few precious rays of the life-giving sun. The canopy of the rainforest was so thick that it was fairly dark under it but Callum still managed to see his hand in front of his face, but they were going to have to be careful here.

The very last thing they wanted was to get ambushed by animals or man-eating plants. He was really hoping Aaron was joking about that little threat.

There were hundreds of roots shooting up out of the ground making each step a difficult harsh mission, because if someone felt and they twisted their ankle then medical help would be hours upon hours away. And in a rainforest you would be dead in those hours.

The deafening sound of primates, insects and snakes made Callum smile because this was such an amazing place. Even the air smelt so much more refreshing, damp and filled with life compared to normal Empire recycled air. This was a version of heaven that Callum seriously didn't want to leave, especially as the taste of summer picnics formed on his tongue just like how he used to have them with his university friends.

"Wow," Aaron said.

Callum loved seeing Aaron so happy and he looked so cute when he was lost in thought and his mind was probably racing as he analysed all the processes happening here.

And Callum wasn't ashamed at all to admit that Aaron still looked so divine in his white shirt, black jeans and hiking boots. They were a new set of clothing to yesterday but that certainly didn't make him look any less attractive.

"Where do we begin?" Callum asked Luna.

Luna passed him and Aaron a large black scanning device in the shape of a dataslate. Callum tapped the screen and it started scanning for any signs of interference.

"Each of our scans are scanning for things that we're experts in," Eli said. "Yours Callum is searching for any signs of geographical interference. Like a process that shouldn't have happened here, something that isn't natural or maybe a magnetic problem,"

Callum nodded. The entire key to terraforming was to basically rewrite the geographical and biological processes of a planet to match those of Earth. And actually now that Eli had gotten him thinking this planet should have been a lot drier.

Terraforma was a little too close to the sun compared to Earth so it should have been dry and not able to support life. Clearly the Terraforming technology had worked that well, so it still made no sense why the Empire stopped using the technology.

Callum started walking through the rainforest making sure he was careful not to trip and break an ankle.

He kept scanning the plants and trees and

ground in hope of finding something. He knew that Luna was following his trail searching for something else and Aaron and Eli were elsewhere.

Callum looked up at the sky and realised that the trees were all slightly bent in the wrong fashion.

He held up his scanner and calculated the angle of the trees and what they should actually be. Everyone knew that plants grow towards the light and on this planet they should have grown at an angle of 12 degrees but the trees were growing straight up regardless of where the light source was coming from.

That should have been impossible and the terraforming technology clearly didn't recreate all of Earth's processes perfectly.

Then again Callum didn't understand why that would matter at all. It didn't really change anything if the trees and plants didn't grow straight or bend or whatever. It wouldn't have harmed humans living here so that was sadly yet another dead end.

Callum kept walking through the forest and the rainforest roots were a lot thicker here and a lot more bendy so it was a lot more difficult for Callum to climb over them. He managed just about.

After a few moments he went up to the edge of a little stream that was flowing fast in the rainforest. It wasn't a stream in the strictest of senses because this was more likely to be just a stream of water run-off but it looked like a stream. And it certainly had the power of one.

Callum pressed the dataslate against the top of

the water and analysed the water content. And it was exactly as it should be and it was perfectly safe, drinkable and wasn't polluted in the slightest.

The stream curved, bend and eroded the rainforest a little but it was just as it should have been. It was just water flowing and doing what it did best by providing a life-giving fluid to the rainforest.

Thunder clouds roared overhead and Callum started to make his way back over to the others so Eli could give him a rain shield like he had offered earlier.

And as Callum kept climbing over the roots to get back, he was starting to get even more fascinated by the mystery of the terraforming because everything looked so perfect here in the rainforest.

So he couldn't help but wonder if everything was just a little too perfect?

CHAPTER 7

Aaron seriously couldn't believe just how humid it was in the rainforest. He had never had his clothes stick to him as much as they were now, and when he had mentioned it earlier to sexy Callum he hadn't even noticed. That was just remarkable to Aaron and it went to show how dedicated Callum was to his work.

A very attractive quality indeed.

As the rain continued to slash, lash and pound the rainforest with more and more little streams carving their way through the forest floor Aaron, Eli and the others kept working their way through the rainforest.

They stepped over immense branches, roots and plants that even snarled at them as they passed but Aaron knew that the very large spiky plant with the red flower to their left wasn't going to strike at them. As long as they didn't get too close actually.

Aaron was more than grateful for the amazing

weather shields that hummed around them and it stopped the rain from pounding on them and chipping away their morale.

The temperature was still boiling hot which was great but it really didn't help the damn humidity. It was still way too hot, sticky and not in the way that Aaron normally liked those two things.

But Callum did look beautiful with his white t-shirt and shorts that clung on him (just like how Aaron wanted to cling to him) and his hiking boots revealing just how fit and well-muscled Callum's legs really were.

"This is the exact centre of the rainforest," Eli said as they came out into a very minor clearing.

Aaron wasn't a fan of calling this a clearing because it was literally a one-metre-squared gap in the rainforest where they were no trees, plants or roots. Granted that was major for a rainforest but it wasn't exactly shouting *clearing* to Aaron.

Anyway, Aaron knew he had more important things to concern himself with so he got out his dataslate and started scanning the plants at the very edge of the "clearing". They were hoping to find some evidence of the terraforming technology.

Aaron wasn't too hopeful because the entire rainforest seemed to be thriving, overtaking land at an impossible rate and it was so alive that he guessed if he placed his dataslate on the ground and left and came back a day later. His dataslate would be completely encased in plants.

Because that was the magical thing about rainforests they were basically mother nature incarnate. And she always claimed her territory no matter how advanced a civilisation got.

Aaron focused on a very beautiful rose-like plant that instead of having thorns had daggers on its side that dripped blood. It was certainly fresh so some poor animal must have attacked it recently and paid the price for its hunger.

His dataslate beeped a little and Aaron rolled his eyes when he saw that there was nothing even remotely strange about the flora of this area. Of course, like sexy Callum had mentioned earlier all the plants were growing perfectly straight but that was the only problem with the plants of this area.

And there was no sign of technology here. Not a dataslate (besides theirs), not a single teleportation imprint (very strange for the Empire) and there wasn't a single sign of human life in the rainforest besides theirs.

There was nothing wrong whatsoever with the rainforest and this might have been the oldest environment on the planet but this wasn't where the terraforming technology had started nor where it was based.

Aaron turned to sexy Callum, Eli and Luna. "Are we assuming the terraforming technology is still on the planet to help regulate the environments and more?"

"Of course," Luna said. "Terraforma couldn't be

left to its own devices because its proximity to the sun would turn most of the planet into a desert,"

Aaron nodded. He had known that but he just wanted to be sure.

They had been searching the rainforest for hours now, scanning trees, plants and even the odd animal that dared itself to get close enough for a detailed scan.

There were no results that supported the idea of terraforming technology being in the rainforest and that just annoyed Aaron. But it also made him smile, a lot.

It was starting to get clearer to him that whoever was in charge of terraforming the planet they clearly wanted the technology to remain hidden and that meant their plan had no sense.

"How about we don't go to the other two biomes?" Aaron asked. If the rainforest was the oldest environment and they hadn't found any evidence of terraforming technology then he seriously doubted they would in the forests and deserts.

Eli slowly nodded. "What do you have in mind? We honestly want both of your perspectives on this because we cannot figure this out ourselves,"

"I'm just thinking that if I was a Terraformer I wouldn't set up my technology and the control centre in some strange isolated environment like a rainforest, forest or desert. What if it went wrong? what if I needed to shut it down?"

Callum hugged Aaron and Aaron groaned by

accident in sheer pleasure from the amazing hug. Everyone laughed.

"I get it," Callum said, "you believe the Terraforming technology is back in the south pole near the resort,"

Aaron wasn't sure if that's what he meant but now Callum had mentioned it the idea seemed perfect and Aaron knew exactly how to build on it.

"Wait. When was the resort built?"

"When Empire forces first… settled on the world," Luna said grinning.

"The resort is the only permeant structure on the entire planet and it's on top of a massive mountain. It would make perfect sense to dig down into the mountain to hide whatever Terraforming tech they needed," Aaron said.

"And only scientists and rich people can go to the resort. It's a perfect cover for people going to fix or monitor or do something to the Terraforming technology without scientists turning up being noticed," Callum said.

Luna grinned at her husband. "I think we need to go back to the resort,"

As they all turned back and started heading towards the shuttles a few hours away, Aaron was so excited about getting one step closer to the truth about Terraforma.

But he still couldn't understand why destroy the terraforming records if the technology was under a resort. It had to be dangerous for the records to be destroyed but it was clearly safe enough to allow a resort to be built on top.

Aaron had no idea what the danger was. Not a clue at all.

CHAPTER 8

Now that they were all back at the resort and hotel, had showers (and Callum so badly wanted to ask Aaron to join him in his shower but he didn't) and Luna had ordered them a quick dinner, they were all back in the conference room and Callum felt so much better now.

It was only in the shower that Callum had realised just how much sweat the humidity had caused him and he somehow hadn't noticed it at all.

As the four of them sat round the silver metal conference table and on the black metal chairs that were a lot colder now than yesterday, Callum really liked the pitch darkness outside that was enlightened with the bright white snow-capped mountains that made the night sky look even more stunning than it normally was. Of course it wasn't as stunning as sexy Aaron who was wearing an untucked white shirt, black jeans and trainers.

He still looked just as beautiful as ever.

Luna and Eli were both wearing some smart-casual business wear and they were organising dataslates in some kind of order that Callum didn't know about. They had been talking, muttering and whispering to each other for a good twenty minutes now and as much as Callum wanted to comment he wanted to let the bright minds work away.

And Callum was thinking about how the terraforming technology might work but it was so advanced he was struggling to make too much progress. It seemed just magical to be able to enhance a planet's geographical forces and bend them to your will creating a brand-new environment.

"Our scans are done," Luna said.

She stood up and a hologram appeared on the conference table showing the entire mountain range in 3D and Callum was more than impressed with some of the stunning tunnels that ran down into the mountains.

Some of those tunnels had to run kilometres down.

"This is the most up-to-update image of the mountain range. It's two months old and this was done from orbit. There are no signs of interference so this is a perfect indication of what the tunnels are like," Luna said.

That was good news at least. Callum was amazed at all the hundreds of tunnels that ran up and down all the mountains. There wasn't a pattern per se but Callum noticed that the air smelt a little off in here.

"Does anyone smell that?" Eli asked.

"Yeah," everyone else said.

Callum was only now starting to understand that it was very musty and the stink of stale air was unbearable but it made no sense. The hotel and resort had access to some of the most advance envirosystems in the Empire.

"Run a scan of the air please," Aaron said. "I know what's going on,"

Luna nodded and Callum wasn't sure but he was surprised when Aaron took his hand and Eli took Luna's. There had to be something going on that Callum wasn't understanding.

"Damn," Luna said. "Oxygen rates are falling across the entire planet. The temperature is rising too,"

"Just as I thought," Aaron said. "The Terraforming technology is failing. The technology that keeps Terraforma at a safe temperature with a working rainforest, desert and all the other environment needed are failing,"

"Wow," Eli said looking at the hologram. "We can't even get off world now because the snow and ice supporting the resort's docking area melted,"

Callum just shook his head. This wasn't what he wanted at all. If that ice had melted then the docking area would have fallen away and there was no Empire Army, Governor or anything to do with the Empire on the planet or even near it.

"Without Empire Government in the region,"

Luna said, "command of a situation falls to the most in charge person here and because we're employed by the Inquisition at the moment that makes me the person in charge,"

That revelation just hung there in the air between them all and Callum didn't know what to say. He held Aaron's hand tighter because he now knew exactly how dangerous this was.

"I'll talk to the hotel manager but we have to find the Terraforming technology now and fix it," Luna said as she got up hugged her husband, kissed him on the lips and waved her goodbyes at Callum and Aaron.

Callum wished he was going with her but Luna was an expert on the politics of management. His expertise laid here in the geographical processes.

Eli swiped at the hologram a few times. "Temperatures could rise as much as 10 degrees in the next day as the terraforming technology fails. That would destroy the rainforests, melt the snow around the resort and the resort could collapse,"

"And kill everyone inside," Callum said.

"Exactly," Eli said. "I'll get the synthesisers to make us a lot of coffee. We have to solve this tonight,"

Callum just nodded and the very idea of the entire planet failing and reverting to a husk of a wasteland scared him a lot more than he ever wanted to admit.

And the thought of all those people dying scared

him even more.

CHAPTER 9

Over the past few hours Aaron had tried everything he could possibly think of to try and understand why the hell the terraforming technology was failing now. It made no sense at all because the Empire had tried to terraform the planet exactly a hundred thousand years ago so why was it failing now?

Aaron had first believed there had been some kind of seismic activity that had damaged the technology but beautiful Callum showed him that was impossible because of the technology freezing natural geographical processes.

Then Aaron proposed that perhaps there had been a collapse in one of the mountain tunnels that had damaged the technology but that didn't work either. It turned out the resort had extensive scanners in all the tunnels and none of them had showed even the slightest sign of a rock collapse.

Aaron had then supposed that solar radiation of

all things might have damaged the technology. Again it hadn't. There hadn't been any solar flares hitting Terraforma in over two hundred years.

Aaron just wanted to bury his head in Callum's wonderful shoulders as they both sat next to each other around the conference table, but he had to keep acting professionally just a little longer. He couldn't let his sex drive overtake the sheer importance of this mission.

Eli was "resting his eyes" in another black chair across from them but Aaron didn't mind. He often found that he tended to have his best ideas after a good nap and to be honest it wasn't like there was anything too dramatic happening right in front of them.

"If this failure isn't geographical in nature," Callum asked. "Could this be plant failure?"

Aaron just grinned. That was such a stupid idea it actually could be true and there was a presence for it in the Empire.

"Actually there could be because a few years back I was hired by the Planetary Governor of a world to help them retake a solar power station that had been overrun by a plant,"

"Seriously?"

Aaron nodded. "Yes. The plant seemed to be drawn obsessively to the electricity stored in the power station so it attacked and fed on the power,"

Aaron swiped the hologram a few times and scanned for the plant but nothing happened. There simply wasn't a complete register of plants on the planet's database.

"What do you remember about the plant? What conditions did it grow under?" Callum asked.

Aaron frowned a little. "It's impossible to say really. I only have the one dataset to go from and as you know that isn't enough data to form a conclusion,"

Callum smiled. Aaron really loved that smile.

"I agree but Aaron, we have a resort filled with people that are going to die if the ice under the resort melts. We need something,"

Aaron nodded. "The power station was in a very moderate climate. Not a lot of heat, not a lot of cold or moisture. Probably like a forest sort of climate like Ancient Europe for example,"

Callum pulled the hologram over to him and Aaron loved watching his fingers dance over the holographic keyboard that appeared in front of him.

"Nothing,"

"What?" Aaron asked.

"There are no rainforests or forests left," Callum said. "They're gone,"

Aaron gasped. It had only been about six hours since they learnt about the danger of the technology failing. How could an entire ecosystem be dead in hours?

"Maybe that's the key to this," Aaron said. "The general theory of terraforming technology is that it sends out an endless pulse of energy that controls the environment,"

"So you think because the environments in the north collapsed first that the technology is in the south,"

Aaron nodded. "Can you run, I don't know, some, some sort of scan or programme to calculate the rough position of the technology?"

Callum bit his lip for a moment. "Maybe. I would have to calculate the geographical forces at play, how they would interact with the environment and more but it's doable. It would take hours,"

Aaron laughed. "That means I get to spend more time with you and I would love that idea,"

Callum grinned at Aaron and he loved Callum's wonderful grin and pearly white teeth.

"Me too," Callum said as Aaron moved closer as Callum started talking him through the calculations.

And as much as Aaron grinned, smiled and acted like nothing was wrong in the entire world Aaron hated how his stomach was twisting into a painful knot.

Because if an entire hemisphere of environments could basically collapse in six hours then time was seriously running out for them.

And the lives they wanted to save.

CHAPTER 10

Callum had really enjoyed the past hour with beautiful, sexy and sensational Aaron sitting next to him. Aaron's mind was just so complex and intelligent that Callum was really enjoying listening to his ideas and most importantly what he was thinking about the calculations he was running.

As they both sat around the silver conference table, Callum and Aaron let the calculations and programme run in the background and Callum couldn't deny he was so enjoying being alone with Aaron. Especially with Eli sleeping opposite them.

His little snoring just made Callum laugh a little because he knew that at the end of the day it really was down to him and Aaron to save everyone. Luna was brilliant and so was Eli but they weren't experts like him and Aaron and right now their priorities were on other things.

The hologram buzzed and Callum really hoped the computer programme had found something to help them solve this disaster.

It had.

Callum stood up and paced around the conference table as the hologram changed from one showing Terraforma and how its landscape was dissolving more and more by the minute to one showing the mountain range they were currently in.

And Callum was so amazed when the programme highlighted that blasts of energy were coming out of every single tunnel in the mountains.

"These tunnels aren't natural," Aaron said. "They were made by the tech,"

Callum nodded. He had reached the same conclusion and he was willing to bet anything that these tunnels were isolated from each other.

"I'm scanning them completely," Aaron said.

That was a good idea and Callum was hoping that it would show some kind of massive cavern showing how all tunnels were connected together.

"No data," Aaron said. "If we send in a probe I don't suspect to get it back,"

"Agreed. The terraforming tech must be sending out so much energy that it heats up the tunnel. A probe would probably melt before it got close enough,"

Callum bit his lip as he realised exactly what he was saying. If the tunnels were too hot for them to send a probe into then they were certainly too hot for them to explore alone.

He doubted the resort had any enviro-suits or

one designed to survive extreme heat and judging by the look of horror on Aaron's face he had come to the same conclusion. Damn it. All Callum wanted to do was stop this disaster and he couldn't.

Callum just weakly smiled at the hot beautiful man he was working with. The environment was about to fail and all life would be exterminated in a few hours on the planet.

Callum didn't want Aaron to die. He wanted Aaron to live, have fun and meet an amazing hot man that could show him the galaxy. And Callum really would sacrifice himself for Aaron if he could.

He would do it without a second thought.

"I would do the same for you you know?" Aaron said.

Callum sometimes hated it how similar they were but Aaron was so perfect in his uncrisp white shirt, black jeans and trainers. He was so damn beautiful that Callum had to figure this out to save him. The man he was definitely in love with.

"What about the temperature of the tunnels?" Aaron asked.

Callum clicked his fingers. That was brilliant. That was a sensational idea.

Callum swiped the hologram a few times and double checked the temperatures of all the tunnels in the mountain range. He was so glad that the resort had advanced weather equipment built-in and that it was working perfectly.

They had just assumed that all the tunnels would

be as hot as each other but that wasn't how weather systems worked. And essentially Terraforma was one immensely complex weather system. But these systems always had cold air returning to the source.

"Found it," Callum said as the hologram zoomed in on a single tunnel that was registering temperature as extreme as minus twenty.

"It's on the other side of the mountain range though," Aaron said. "We don't have access to shuttles. There isn't time to hike it. We aren't even expert climbers,"

Callum went to stomp his foot. But he didn't. He knew that Aaron was only trying to keep them realistic and that was getting harder and harder all the time.

"Let's see if the hotel has something we don't know about," Aaron said taking Callum's hand in his.

And as Aaron dragged him out of the conference room Callum just hoped that the hotel and resort did have something they could use.

That tunnel was the only way down into a possible cavern that could save everyone and Callum hated how they knew it existed but they didn't have a way to get to it.

It was mocking them. And Callum hated being mocked by anyone and anything. Including mother nature.

CHAPTER 11

Aaron seriously hadn't realised just how great the air inside the conference room was until he went into the main area of the resort, which was nothing more than a large reception area with a wooden desk, brown wooden walls that made it look like a log cabin from Old Earth and tons of people were sitting on the floor. Fear carved into their faces.

There were so many people here now, the young and older, the under- and overweight and the rich and poor. All sitting on the floor covering themselves in blankets and hoping that Aaron was going to give them good news.

Aaron couldn't see Luna whatsoever but there were so many people here that he wasn't surprised. The air was icy cold and the hints of must, damp and mould filled the air just highlighting how bad the air was failing on the planet.

And it would get worse if they didn't get to that tunnel and descend into the darkness and hopefully they would find the Terraforming technology in a cavern or something.

There was a lot of hoping but Aaron didn't see what other options they had.

"Doctors," Luna said wearing a thick artic blue coat and shivering.

"We need a transport or something. We have a location for the terraforming technology but it's on the other side of the mountain range," Aaron said.

Luna frowned. "That's amazing but we don't have anything. The docking area collapsed. The emergency hangar is flooded with melted snow water and there's nothing left,"

A loud roar ripped through the mountain range and everyone in the reception area screamed. The air became thick choking and Aaron's eyes watered as the smell of rotten eggs filled his senses.

A little old lady came over wearing a thin blue blanket, a skirt and a pearl necklace. "Did I hear that you have a location?"

Aaron didn't see the point in lying to the woman considering they would all probably be dead soon.

"Yes," Callum said. "We just need a way to get there,"

The little old lady smiled. "I might have a way. You see me and my husband first came here when the resort opened all those tens of thousands of years ago,"

Aaron was flat out stunned. She must have had more rejuvenation treatments than legally allowed.

"And once I saw the then-owner go into a private chamber with a teleporter inside," the lady said.

Aaron really hated the idea of teleporting randomly to a tunnel that they didn't know was safe or not. But it was worth a try.

"Do you remember where?" Aaron asked.

"Of course," the lady said.

"Then Callum get the woman to show you where it was," Aaron said before turning to Luna. "We need enviro-suits now please,"

Callum rushed off with the little old lady and Aaron followed Luna behind the wooden desk that had its holographic computers turned off and they looked broken.

As Luna reactivated them with the holograms flashing every so often and humming loudly Aaron leant close to her.

"How is everyone?"

Luna grinned. "Not good. That is a silly question. I've contacted Region Command but they're tens of solar systems away. They won't reach us for months,"

Aaron bit his lip. He hated that information.

"I don't know what else I can do to make them comfortable," Luna said, "and Aaron, I'm scared,"

Aaron smiled because that really drummed home just how bad and apocalyptic the situation was because Luna was a woman of science, logical and rational behaviour.

And she was scared so Aaron was terrified.

"When me and Callum leave. Go and be with your husband. He loves you. Be with him," Aaron said.

Luna swiped the hologram a few times as she smiled. "Who made you so tough and wise all of a sudden?"

"I don't know. Death focuses the mind,"

Luna nodded. "If you fail just kiss Callum before you die. Don't die with any regrets,"

Aaron nodded because it was all he could do. He hadn't thought at all about his own death but she was right. He didn't want to die at all without at least kissing Callum.

The man he loved.

"Found them," Luna said and a wooden panel behind them dissolved revealing two bright yellow enviro-suits.

Aaron grabbed them, hugged Luna and just looked at her a final time just in case they didn't come back.

"The Emperor Protects," Aaron said. It was a famous Empire saying and one that Aaron just wanted to be correct right now.

Luna weakly smiled and Aaron went off to see that Callum was standing in the middle of the corridor standing on some kind of raised metal circular platform.

He had no idea that the little old lady was wrong about the teleporter being in the open.

"I've added the coordinates," the lady said.

Aaron hugged her and passed Callum his enviro-suit and they both put it on without hesitation. Since hesitation was death now.

After they got their enviro-suits on the lady smiled and Aaron blew her a kiss as she activated the teleporter.

And as blue smoke swirled, twirled and whirled around them. Aaron felt the world fall away from him and his stomach twisted as he knew there was only one shot to save everyone.

TERRAFORMA

CHAPTER 12

As soon as Callum rematerialised in front of the immense tunnel opening that was a massive hole in the jet black rock with snow no longer covering the mountain. He realised they didn't bring any climbing equipment or anything.

The immense tunnel went down at a very steep angle and Callum was surprised at the sheer coldness of the mountain air and the tunnel itself. The enviro-suits hummed loudly as the nano-motors struggled and strained to keep their bodies warm.

It was a nightmare and Callum saw that they were standing on the very edge of the mountain with a sheer drop only centimetres away.

Callum took a step closer to the tunnel and he couldn't see anything whatsoever. It was shrouded in pitch darkness and it was impossible to see if there was any sharp rocks that could cut their enviro-suits.

"We have to go down no matter what," Aaron said.

Callum nodded and as Aaron went to go down first he grabbed him and pulled him close.

"Let me go first. If I die then you won't. You'll know to come another way," Aaron said.

"Throne I do love you," Callum said. He was surprised that it didn't feel weird at all rolling off his tongue like it had with so many other guys before.

"I love you too," Aaron said. "I don't want anything bad to happen to you,"

Callum so badly wanted to kiss him but the helmets of their suits made that impossible.

"Then let's make a promise to each other. When we survive this we will go on a date and kiss and have amazing sex. We will be together and have a good time," Callum said.

Aaron looked at the tunnel. "Let's go,"

Callum gasped as Aaron quickly walked down the tunnel and he joined him.

Callum walked as quickly as he could given the danger luring them down there. He couldn't see anything.

The ground felt soft and crumbly. Shards of rock broke off under his feet and Callum almost fell over again and again as the icy cold rocks cracked.

Callum wanted this to be over so he could have fun with Aaron but the mission came first. He felt the cold draft zoom past him.

The edges of the tunnel were especially crumbly and they only seemed to crumble more and more the deeper they got into the tunnel. Then a strange sound of whistling filled the air.

A large chunk of rock hit Callum pushing him forward. It shattered easily on impact but it just went to show that the tunnel wasn't stable at all.

Callum felt his body want to roll forwards at the sheer angle of the tunnel as they descended. He threw his weight backwards to balance it all out.

Another rock smashed into his back almost making Callum lose his balance completely.

Callum kept walking. "Are you okay?"

He didn't hear Aaron at all. He hadn't heard anything but he had been concentrating on not falling himself.

Another rock pounded into his back.

Then another.

Then another.

Callum fell forward.

Zooming down the tunnel as tens of rocks joined him.

Rocks slammed into him.

Callum kept falling. Kept increasing speed. Kept accelerating.

Callum screamed as he plumped towards the bottom.

CHAPTER 13

When Aaron's eyes flickered open the smell of damp, pine and freshly cut rosemary filled his senses. It was one of the best smells he had ever had the pleasure of smelling and that was exactly how he knew that something was awfully wrong.

Aaron forced himself up and he bit his lip when he saw he was in a large rock cavern easily big enough to fit ten maybe twenty football stadiums in from Old Earth. It was so immense in scale that Aaron could barely see the top of the black rock walls and cavern.

All the cavern walls and ceiling were covered in bright pink glowing crystals that shone so bright Aaron was fairly sure they were never going to need lighting in the cavern and that's when he saw the source of so much life and so much death.

Right in the middle of the cavern there was a massive holographic computer terminal that was deactivated but it had its grey metal dome on the floor and a small opening at the top to allow a hologram to peek through.

The dome didn't seem to be connected to anything else but as Aaron went over to it. He could feel how churned up, damaged and wrecked the rocky floor was. Clearly there were some cables, tubes or something else underneath the ground.

"So this is it?" Callum asked.

Aaron hugged him. He was so glad Callum was alive after he had fallen. Those rocks were strangely soft and they had attacked them out of nowhere.

Aaron and Callum went over to the metal dome that Aaron was now realising came up to his waist. The dome seemed so unimportant but that was probably by design.

The sheer heat and lack of humidity annoyed Aaron. He felt as if he was standing in a desert but that didn't explain the damp smell.

"Something's very wrong here," Callum said and Aaron went over to him because he was now on the other side of the metal dome.

Aaron gasped when he saw that a large brown plant root had smashed its way into the metal dome.

"That's the plant I was talking about," Aaron said. "This is the plant that attacked that power station but this is on a lot smaller scale,"

"Does it matter? This plant is still causing so much damage,"

"Incorrect," a computerised voice said as a large golden hologram popped out the top of the metal dome.

Aaron smiled when he saw it was a very tall holographic woman with brown skin, a wonderful smile and a long dress that flattered her figure.

"I have been waiting for you for a long time doctors," the hologram said. "My name is… oh, I do not know my name anymore. I must add that to…"

Aaron just bit his lip as he saw how annoyed and sad and frustrated the hologram was that it was forgetting basic things. The hologram was probably some form of artificial intelligence, something that was now outlawed in the Empire.

"Explain what's happening," Callum said.

The AI grinned. "You as expected Doctor, over time Mother Nature would seek to reclaim her world. It was small at first a tree dying here and there. A few thousand cattle dying of a disease and then the humans started disappearing,"

Aaron shook his head. This wasn't right at all.

"The world started turning against itself. As you suggested and programmed me Doctor, I tried to counter all these measures. But Mother Nature was patient. I'm decaying my code is fading away and my, memory, I think I got it right is dying,"

Aaron nodded as he realised what was actually going on here. And this is why the Empire had stopped terraforming because the Empire must have learnt that it was impossible to control entire planets and force their geographical processes to act a certain way.

Aaron had once had a discussion with an ex-boyfriend about terraforming and the damn ex was right now. Because as he said a planet is like a child you can guide it, help it and support it. But if you control the child then you will create a monster. Aaron hated him being right.

"Complete system malfunction will happen in thirty minutes," the AI said. "We must-"

Then the hologram died and the glowing crystals on the walls crackled a little.

"We have to solve this," Callum said. "And we are the only two people that can,"

Aaron wanted to agree with him but he just had no idea how. This was impossible.

"Aaron come on. We are both experts and there must be a way to reboot this system enough to at least buy us enough time for an evacuation,"

"Okay. We need to reactivate the terraforming technology and somehow get it working again,"

Aaron started tapping the cold metal dome in hope of finding some kind of access hatch that would allow him to see the hologram's code. He wasn't a programmer but he once dated a man that was.

That had to be good enough for now.

After a few moments of searching Aaron found a very small metal panel that popped up. It was no larger than his hand but he had to try something.

When him and Callum got the panel open he bit his lip in frustration because there was nothing there. No way to access computer systems or holograms or anything.

It was only a bunch of burnt away wires.

Aaron just looked at Callum. They only had thirty minutes to save the world and they had no idea how to do it.

CHAPTER 14

They only had twenty minutes left before the entire ecosystem of Terraforma utterly failed and Callum seriously hated that idea but it was the situation they were in and now he just had to fix it.

Considering all environmental systems were mixtures of geographical processes he knew that he was the one that needed to come up with some idea.

It was so annoying that as he stood in a beautiful cavern with bright pink crystals glowing on the walls. He just couldn't think of an idea whatsoever. Everyone was going to die because of him.

"The terraforming technology's failure means environmental systems cannot be maintained," Aaron said.

Callum just clicked his fingers. He was so going to reward and do Aaron very well later.

It made perfect sense that the Terraforming technology was only one thing. Of course it was made up of two stages. The first stage of the technology was to create the various environments in the first place, then the second stage of the tech was to maintain them.

Not continuously recreate brand-new environments.

"The air system. We first noticed the tunnels because of the hot and cold air around the mountain range,"

Aaron nodded.

Callum really wished he had seen it sooner.

"In geography the hot air creates high pressure and cold air creates low pressure. It is that pressure system that creates weather and helps to maintain environments,"

"So you want to kickstart the process again?"

"Yes," Callum said. "If we create a massive blast of hot air that would have the power to kickstart the weather system again. It would launch hot air out towards the desert and rainforest systems bringing out cold air towards the mountain range,"

"And stop the ice under the resort melting,"

"Exactly," Callum said.

Callum just looked at the metal dome. He had no idea how but they were going to have to cause an explosion.

He went over to the cavern's black walls and looked at the pink glowing crystals. There was a chance that these crystals were glowing because of heat and other chemical reactions.

Callum kicked one.

Aaron tackled him.

Boiling hot steam rushed out. The temperature rose dramatically. Sweat poured off Callum.

Callum nodded that was good. He looked at Aaron and both of them grinned.

If his calculations were right there were more than enough crystals in the chamber to cause a massive unleash of hot air through the tunnel network.

Callum started to kick more crystals. Aaron helped him. The temperature got hotter and hotter.

Callum wiped more and more sweat off his head. His clothes were soaked through. He had no idea how Aaron managed in his white shirt.

He realised their enviro-suits had failed and melted open.

"Stop," Callum said through the hissing of steam shooting out of the walls.

Callum went over to Aaron and got him to stop. There was a problem. They were both already sweating too much for this to be safe.

His throat was as dry as a desert and Callum just felt so ill. The chamber was so hot but he knew that it wasn't hot enough to reverse the damage of terraforming technology failing.

And if they continued then things would only get worse and there was a good chance they would die from heat stroke before the mission was done.

Callum leant on the increasingly annoying metal dome.

"There has to be a way to destroy the crystals all at once," Aaron said.

Callum shrugged. It was way too hot to think here but beautiful Aaron had a point.

Callum went back over to the access panel that Aaron had found earlier and really looked at it. There were so many burnt wires in there but it was so cool as well.

He stuck his hand inside and it was so cold compared to the air that Callum hissed in pain.

"Get me a crystal," Callum said.

Aaron nodded and ran away.

Callum was so glad that Aaron wasn't questioning him here. All that Callum wanted to do was throw in a boiling hot crystal in hope of catching the entire thing on fire.

Then hopefully the fire inside the metal dome would cause an explosion of some kind.

Callum moved out the way and Aaron threw it into the metal dome.

Callum closed the access panel but he heard the crystal hiss and fizz out.

"And how would we escape?" Aaron asked.

Callum was hardly impressed that Aaron must have given him a cooled crystal because it didn't work. But it was a good point.

If the metal dome did explode then would there actually be time to run away and escape?

Callum ran to the other side of the cavern. He looked up at the large tunnel they had fallen down from and it was too steep to climb up quickly.

Callum shrugged and he felt Aaron hug him.

"We have to do this you know," Aaron said. "If we have to die so all those people in the hotel can live. I'm okay with that. I would prefer you not being here with me but I'm glad that I got to tell you I love you,"

Callum grinned. It was the truth and Callum felt the same way but there was no way in hell Callum was dying here today.

And he certainly wasn't allowing Aaron to die either. He was working to make Aaron go out on a date with him and dying in a fiery blaze wasn't going to be an excuse for them not going out.

Callum just had to find out a way for them to escape.

CHAPTER 15

Aaron seriously couldn't believe the stupid temperature in the cavern as it just kept rising and rising and the two of them couldn't escape. Callum was still pacing around but they only had ten minutes left until Terraforma fell to mother nature.

Aaron couldn't imagine the sheer power of nature until now. And because of human arrogance they were going to die a very painful death.

Unless Aaron could somehow figure out a way for them to escape. It was impossible to find let alone climb one of the hot tunnels that carried boiling hot air of the terraforming technology. They would be cooked alive and they couldn't climb the cold tunnel they had come down from. It was too steep and there would be so much cold air returning it would blow them back down into the annihilated cavern.

Or maybe they could survive it?

Aaron went over to Callum. "I have a new plan. If you give me a leg up so I can reach the lip of the tunnel we came down. You throw a crystal into the metal dome and I'll pull you up,"

Callum didn't seem sure.

"Then we start climbing. The explosion will happen and the air will rush out of the hot tunnels and we kept climbing,"

"And you think there'll be so much cold air when it returns even if it blows us back down the coldness of the air will take the heat away from the fire and stop it,"

Aaron nodded. That was the extremely vain hope anyway.

The temperature increased even more and Aaron just went over to the edge of the cavern and jumped up so his fingers barely caught the edge of the tunnel lip.

Callum thankfully came over and helped him up.

Once Aaron was on the lip of the tunnel he tried to look up but he couldn't make out anything. There was a bright light of the outside high above but he couldn't make out the edges of the tunnel.

They would be doing this completely and utterly blind.

Aaron looked down at the man he loved and nodded.

Then crouched down so he could pull Callum up the moment he was ready and hopefully before the cavern exploded.

"The Emperor Protects," Aaron said quietly hoping that stupid Empire saying would work.

Aaron nodded. Callum nodded. It was game time.

Callum rushed over to a wall. He broke off a crystal and ran over to the access panel. Throwing the crystal inside.

Callum rushed over to the wall and jumped into the air. Aaron grabbed his hand and pulled him up.

Both of them started climbing. The rock was too soft. It was falling away from them rapidly.

It was like climbing up on a down escalator.

Crackling filled the chamber. A surge of adrenaline filled Aaron's body and he shot forward.

He started climbing. Faster and faster.

He didn't have time to see if Callum was behind him. He kept climbing.

Aaron felt his enviro-suit reactivate. It was shielding him from the heat.

The enviro-suit allowed his hands to become sticky. Aaron climbed even faster now.

A deafening explosion ripped through the cavern. The entire cavern screamed in rage as the explosion annihilated it.

Aaron kept climbing.

Dust and rocks and more debris rushed past. The enviro-suit roared in protest.

The shockwave ripped through the tunnel carrying Aaron forward rapidly.

He couldn't see anything. He felt rock hit his skin. He didn't know if he was going to be fired like a cannon out of the tunnel's mouth.

And down toward the mountain floor kilometres below.

Sunlight filled his vision.

Aaron screamed. He was falling through the air.

He was plumping towards the ground. He couldn't see the tunnel's mouth anymore.

Aaron was going to die. He didn't want to die.

Swirls twirls and whirls of blue smoke wrapped around Aaron and he felt his entire body faint from shock.

And his entire world turned black.

CHAPTER 16

When Callum rematerialised back in the large reception area of the resort with its wonderful log cabin walls, wooden desk and delightful people walking about like there was nothing wrong, he was so glad that everything had worked out okay and that Terraforma hadn't died just yet.

There were plenty of people still in the reception area but they weren't covered up with blankets. Some of them were wearing dresses, suits and casual business wear because they knew that the threat was over. And actually Callum was really pleased that the entire atmosphere felt so much calmer, happier and relaxed compared to when he had left.

Luna and Eli were talking to the little old lady from earlier and those three had to be the only people who were having a serious conversation. Everyone else was smiling, cheering and most of them were actually lunch. It was remarkable that everyone was okay.

Callum just grinned like a little schoolboy when Aaron rematerialised next to him and Aaron just leant against him. His white shirt, black jeans and hiking boots were a mess. He was clearly fatigued but Callum didn't mind that, he was as well. And all that Callum wanted to do was sleep with the beautiful man that he seriously loved.

Callum helped Aaron slowly over to Luna and Eli and that's when he noticed the little old lady was grinning like she was about to announce something so marvellous that Callum was going to be delighted. He seriously doubted that.

"My ship will arrive in the next two hours to help get these people off the planet," the little old lady said.

And Callum just looked at her. "You aren't a little old lady are you?"

The woman laughed. "Of course. Yet I am also Inquisitor Serenity and I am the one that hired you and I kept my ship close-ish to make sure nothing went wrong,"

Callum just shook his head because this was so typical of the Inquisition but Callum also knew that because her ship was delayed, it was still him and Aaron that had saved everyone, and managed to buy enough time for the ship to arrive.

"Thank you for emergency teleportation of our friends," Eli said.

Serenity gave him a mocking bow. "Their knowledge is useless to me dead so I require their lives and I would like to see your research in a few days please,"

"I presume you're going to take away the offer of allowing us to publish our research," Callum said.

The silence that hung between the five of them was immense and Callum was fairly sure he could cut it with a knife.

All of them were relying on them being able to publish their research for the sake of their careers. If they didn't publish or show their findings then it was one less credit to their name and the less credits a person had the less likely they were to get academic work again.

"Of course not," Serenity said. "I hired you all for a reason and you have saved all these lives including my own. I will however place an Inquisitorial Merit on all your articles,"

Callum coughed and Aaron just hugged him tighter. No one got a Merit easily and it was such an amazing symbol of a researcher's work that it was even better than anything the Inquisition could have done themselves.

It was such a privilege and powerful mark that Callum didn't even know what to compare it to.

"And now my friends I must go and tell the guests here to prepare for immediate departure when my ship arrives," Serenity said.

Without even giving them time to save goodbye, she left and Callum just looked at the stunning man he had fallen for so much during this wonderful trip.

The trip where he had fallen in love, learnt so many amazing things about the Empire and now he was going to have the career he had always wanted.

A career where everyone knew exactly how great of a researcher he was and that he would be recorded in history as one of the Greatest Researchers of the modern age.

In a way it was sort of the dream for all researchers and academics and until now, Callum had no idea that was what he wanted but now he had. And now he had it with the love of his life standing next to him, Callum was seriously looking forward to the future of his relationship, his career and his knowledge.

And as much as Callum didn't want to get excited about things that hadn't happened yet, he just knew without a shadow of a doubt that he was going to have a boyfriend and their love would turn to marriage in short order, his career would continue to take him to amazing worlds with his wonderful husband Aaron by his side and he would always treasure his delightful friendship with Luna and Eli.

The two people that had made all of this possible.

"Let's grab lunch before we go," Callum said.

"No. Forget lunch. I want the Emperor's Breakfast. It might be the last time I have it," Aaron said.

As the four of them laughed their way out onto the deck Callum just kissed and hugged the man he loved because life was amazing and he wouldn't change any of it for a single moment.

CHAPTER 17

Even now Aaron couldn't believe how kind Inquisitor Serenity had been to allow him and Callum to watch the failure of the terraforming technology from the bridge of her ship (a name she still wouldn't tell them) and as Aaron and Callum stood on the small circular chamber without any walls and was only covered in glass windows, he just stared out at the stunning planet of Terraforma.

It was amazing how the planet still looked like Earth even now with its immense deserts around the central regions, the snow covered north and south poles and the endless forests claiming the upper north and south regions. It actually didn't look too much like modern Earth but Aaron had been privileged enough to see real pictures of Earth from the days of Old Earth.

It was so stunning and Earth really was a beautiful planet, and now Terraforma was going to die and become what it was always meant to be.

Aaron had already watched the oceans get boiled away and the clouds had rained as quickly as they had formed but the ground was probably so hot, it simply boiled away again and again. Terraforma was never meant to have oceans and Aaron fully believed in a year, ten years or hundred years Terraforma would recover completely.

The air was cold with hints of sweat, burnt oil and burnt ozone that wasn't unpleasant but it just reminded Aaron of what they would have to witness. The Empire didn't have any beautiful worlds that a normal person could witness, and even Terraforma wasn't one of them. It was only the rich-rich and the scientists that could go there.

And at first Aaron hadn't agreed with that policy at all but now he understood, no one in Empire Government wanted innocent people to die when the Terraforming technology failed outright. And they probably believed in they allowed scientists to go there then it would have been fine in the end.

Aaron just shook his head and hugged Callum even tighter and at least they had saved everyone from dying a horrible death. He didn't know how long the Empire had known about the failure of the Terraforming technology but he believed it was from the beginning.

Because as much as Aaron studied, worked with and modified plants, the truth was Mother Nature reclaimed everything in the end. You could work with her, modify her and ask her nicely to change a thing or two but you could never control her.

Terraforma was proof of that and when the planet finally broke and all the high-pressure air that Aaron and Callum had kicked into the planet's atmosphere had failed. He was shocked.

It was like the strangest explosion Aaron had ever seen ripped through the planet like a shockwave.

The mountains in the south turned grey all of a sudden as millions of litres of ice, snow and rocks were melted and chipped. The mountains exploded and millions of years of geographical processes screamed back to life.

The mountains were levelled in a second. The mountains that never should have been there were gone in a second.

The shockwave seemed to smash into the bare oceans and vaporise all the coral, sea life and all the organisms that once called the dead ocean home were all gone.

They were erased from history just like the Empire had tried to erase Mother Nature.

When the shockwave hit the desert Aaron was surprised nothing seemed to happen but then the deserts turned a deep shade of red. Million and billions and trillions of grains of sand were compressed together and formed solid land. And that was that. Land that hadn't been solid since Terraforma's discovery was now solid once more.

It was amazing to watch as the rainforests and forests were reduced to ash, every tree was atomised and every single living thing on the planet died.

Death was the only result when Mother Nature was controlled. She might have been a creator of life but she was also a mass murderer and Aaron understood that now.

The Terraforma was reduced to nothing but a wasteland Aaron now understood exactly why he had wanted to do this job in the first place. It was because he wanted to understand nature at a deep level, he honestly thought he understood it inside and out but it was only now that he truly understood the sheer power of the plants he studied.

And he was proud of it.

As Callum kissed him and hugged him and made Aaron feel loved for the first time in a very, very long time, Aaron just knew that everything would be okay. The people were safe, their careers were more than secure and now they had each other.

Callum might have studied geography instead of plants but Aaron didn't care about that. Callum was a strong, beautiful man that Aaron was looking forward to spending the rest of his life with, exploring the Empire and continuing their studies.

They were both workaholics and Aaron loved that about Callum, but there was a promise they had made to each other and Aaron was more than determined to make good on it.

"Come on then," Aaron said pulling Callum close. "We have a night of dating, kissing and maybe something more,"

Callum grinned. "Will I get to take you out of that shirt, jeans and boots later on?"

Aaron shrugged like that was an impossibility but they both just smiled like too loved-up scientists because that's exactly what they were. They had both been through the impossible with each other, bonded like no one could and they would going to have a wonderful life together.

A wonderful life that Aaron was so excited about was going to start right now and never end.

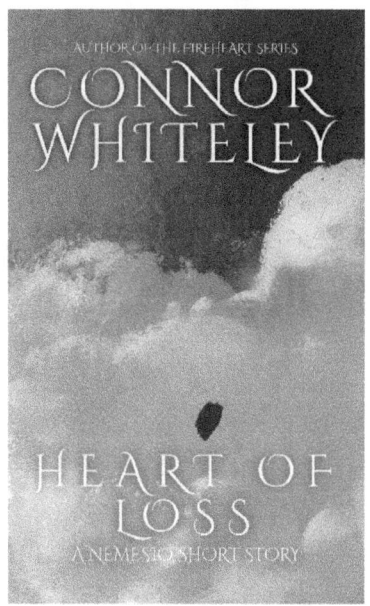

GET YOUR FREE AND EXCLUSIVE SHORT STORY NOW! LEARN ABOUT NEMESIO'S PAST!

https://www.subscribepage.com/fireheart

Keep up to date with exclusive deals on Connor Whiteley's Books, as well as the latest news about new releases and so much more!

Sign up for the Grab a Book and Chill Monthly newsletter, and you'll get one **FREE** ebook just for signing up: Agents of The Emperor Collection.

Sign Up Now!

https://dl.bookfunnel.com/f4p5xkprbk

About the author:

Connor Whiteley is the author of over 60 books in the sci-fi fantasy, nonfiction psychology and books for writer's genre and he is a Human Branding Speaker and Consultant.

He is a passionate warhammer 40,000 reader, psychology student and author.

Who narrates his own audiobooks and he hosts The Psychology World Podcast.

All whilst studying Psychology at the University of Kent, England.

Also, he was a former Explorer Scout where he gave a speech to the Maltese President in August 2018 and he attended Prince Charles' 70th Birthday Party at Buckingham Palace in May 2018.

Plus, he is a self-confessed coffee lover!

OTHER SHORT STORIES BY CONNOR WHITELEY

<u>Mystery Short Story Collections</u>
Criminally Good Stories Volume 1: 20 Detective Mystery Short Stories
Criminally Good Stories Volume 2: 20 Private Investigator Short Stories
Criminally Good Stories Volume 3: 20 Crime Fiction Short Stories
Criminally Good Stories Volume 4: 20 Science Fiction and Fantasy Mystery Short Stories
Criminally Good Stories Volume 5: 20 Romantic Suspense Short Stories

<u>Mystery Short Stories:</u>
Protecting The Woman She Hated
Finding A Royal Friend
Our Woman In Paris
Corrupt Driving
A Prime Assassination
Jubilee Thief
Jubilee, Terror, Celebrations
Negative Jubilation
Ghostly Jubilation
Killing For Womenkind
A Snowy Death

Miracle Of Death
A Spy In Rome
The 12:30 To St Pancreas
A Country In Trouble
A Smokey Way To Go
A Spicy Way To GO
A Marketing Way To Go
A Missing Way To Go
A Showering Way To Go
Poison In The Candy Cane
Christmas Innocence
You Better Watch Out
Christmas Theft
Trouble In Christmas
Smell of The Lake
Problem In A Car
Theft, Past and Team
Embezzler In The Room
A Strange Way To Go
A Horrible Way To Go
Ann Awful Way To Go
An Old Way To Go
A Fishy Way To Go
A Pointy Way To Go
A High Way To Go
A Fiery Way To Go
A Glassy Way To Go

A Chocolatey Way To Go
Kendra Detective Mystery Collection Volume 1
Kendra Detective Mystery Collection Volume 2
Stealing A Chance At Freedom
Glassblowing and Death
Theft of Independence
Cookie Thief
Marble Thief
Book Thief
Art Thief
Mated At The Morgue
The Big Five Whoopee Moments
Stealing An Election
Mystery Short Story Collection Volume 1
Mystery Short Story Collection Volume 2
Criminal Performance
Candy Detectives
Key To Birth In The Past

Science Fiction Short Stories:
Temptation
Superhuman Autospy
Blood In The Redwater
All Is Dust
Vigil

TERRAFORMA

Emperor Forgive Us
Their Brave New World
Gummy Bear Detective
The Candy Detective
What Candies Fear
The Blurred Image
Shattered Legions
The First Rememberer
Life of A Rememberer
System of Wonder
Lifesaver
Remarkable Way She Died
The Interrogation of Annabella Stormic
Blade of The Emperor
Arbiter's Truth
Computation of Battle
Old One's Wrath
Puppets and Masters
Ship of Plague
Interrogation
Edge of Failure
One Way Choice
Acceptable Losses
Balance of Power
Good Idea At The Time
Escape Plan
Escape In The Hesitation

Inspiration In Need
Singing Warriors
Knowledge is Power
Killer of Polluters
Climate of Death
The Family Mailing Affair
Defining Criminality
The Martian Affair
A Cheating Affair
The Little Café Affair
Mountain of Death
Prisoner's Fight
Claws of Death
Bitter Air
Honey Hunt
Blade On A Train

<u>Fantasy Short Stories:</u>
City of Snow
City of Light
City of Vengeance
Dragons, Goats and Kingdom
Smog The Pathetic Dragon
Don't Go In The Shed
The Tomato Saver
The Remarkable Way She Died
The Bloodied Rose
Asmodia's Wrath

Heart of A Killer
Emissary of Blood
Dragon Coins
Dragon Tea
Dragon Rider
Sacrifice of the Soul
Heart of The Flesheater
Heart of The Regent
Heart of The Standing
Feline of The Lost
Heart of The Story
City of Fire
Awaiting Death

Other books by Connor Whiteley:

Bettie English Private Eye Series
A Very Private Woman
The Russian Case
A Very Urgent Matter
A Case Most Personal
Trains, Scots and Private Eyes
The Federation Protects

Lord of War Origin Trilogy:
Not Scared Of The Dark
Madness
Burn Them All

The Fireheart Fantasy Series
Heart of Fire
Heart of Lies
Heart of Prophecy
Heart of Bones
Heart of Fate

City of Assassins (Urban Fantasy)
City of Death
City of Marytrs
City of Pleasure
City of Power

Agents of The Emperor
Return of The Ancient Ones
Vigilance
Angels of Fire
Kingmaker
The Eight
The Lost Generation
Hunt
Emperor's Council
Speaker of Treachery
Birth Of The Empire
Terraforma

Lord Of War Trilogy (Agents of The Emperor)
Not Scared Of The Dark
Madness
Burn It All Down

The Garro Series- Fantasy/Sci-fi
GARRO: GALAXY'S END
GARRO: RISE OF THE ORDER
GARRO: END TIMES
GARRO: SHORT STORIES
GARRO: COLLECTION
GARRO: HERESY
GARRO: FAITHLESS

GARRO: DESTROYER OF WORLDS
GARRO: COLLECTIONS BOOK 4-6
GARRO: MISTRESS OF BLOOD
GARRO: BEACON OF HOPE
GARRO: END OF DAYS

Winter Series- Fantasy Trilogy Books
WINTER'S COMING
WINTER'S HUNT
WINTER'S REVENGE
WINTER'S DISSENSION

Miscellaneous:
RETURN
FREEDOM
SALVATION
Reflection of Mount Flame
The Masked One
The Great Deer

Gay Romance Novellas
Breaking, Nursing, Repairing A Broken Heart
Jacob And Daniel
Fallen For A Lie
Spying And Weddings

TERRAFORMA

All books in 'An Introductory Series':
Careers In Psychology
Psychology of Suicide
Dementia Psychology
Forensic Psychology of Terrorism And Hostage-Taking
Forensic Psychology of False Allegations
Year In Psychology
BIOLOGICAL PSYCHOLOGY 3RD EDITION
COGNITIVE PSYCHOLOGY THIRD EDITION
SOCIAL PSYCHOLOGY- 3RD EDITION
ABNORMAL PSYCHOLOGY 3RD EDITION
PSYCHOLOGY OF RELATIONSHIPS- 3RD EDITION
DEVELOPMENTAL PSYCHOLOGY 3RD EDITION
HEALTH PSYCHOLOGY
RESEARCH IN PSYCHOLOGY
A GUIDE TO MENTAL HEALTH AND TREATMENT AROUND THE WORLD- A GLOBAL LOOK AT DEPRESSION
FORENSIC PSYCHOLOGY
THE FORENSIC PSYCHOLOGY OF THEFT, BURGLARY AND OTHER

CRIMES AGAINST PROPERTY
CRIMINAL PROFILING: A FORENSIC PSYCHOLOGY GUIDE TO FBI PROFILING AND GEOGRAPHICAL AND STATISTICAL PROFILING.
CLINICAL PSYCHOLOGY
FORMULATION IN PSYCHOTHERAPY
PERSONALITY PSYCHOLOGY AND INDIVIDUAL DIFFERENCES
CLINICAL PSYCHOLOGY REFLECTIONS VOLUME 1
CLINICAL PSYCHOLOGY REFLECTIONS VOLUME 2
Clinical Psychology Reflections Volume 3
CULT PSYCHOLOGY
Police Psychology

A Psychology Student's Guide To University
How Does University Work?
A Student's Guide To University And Learning
University Mental Health and Mindset

www.ingramcontent.com/pod-product-compliance
Lightning Source LLC
LaVergne TN
LVHW012121070526
838202LV00056B/5815